Token Wishes

by Bobbi JG Weiss & David Cody Weiss

Illustrated by Piero Piluso

SCHOLASTIC INC.

New York   Toronto   London   Auckland   Sydney
Mexico City   New Delhi   Hong Kong   Buenos Aires

Published by Scholastic Inc.,
90 Old Sherman Turnpike, Danbury, Connecticut 06816.

SCHOLASTIC and associated logos are trademarks
and/or registered trademarks of Scholastic Inc.

ISBN 0-439-56269-4

First Scholastic Printing, September 2003

Chapters

Chapter 1
A Fairy Happy Job

One day, Timmy Turner was playing his new *Action Surgery!* game when his fairy godparents, Cosmo and Wanda, appeared.

"Guess what, Timmy?" said Cosmo. "We're leaving!"

"WHAT?!" cried Timmy.

"Our wands are in the shop for their 50,000-wish tune-up," explained Wanda. "We don't have any extra magic today."

"That's right!" said Cosmo. "So we decided to take a vacation at the Six Wands Fairy

Resort! There's golf! Tennis! Swimming! And lots of fatty foods to eat!"

"But what if I need to make a wish?" Timmy asked.

"TA-DA-A-A!" said Cosmo and Wanda together. "Wish Tokens!"

"Wish Tokens?" Timmy asked.

"Each star inside will grant you one wish," Wanda explained. "It's our job to make sure you're happy, you know."

"Even if we're off having a really good time somewhere else!" added Cosmo.

"Wish Tokens," thought Timmy as his fairy godparents disappeared. "Cool! I'm set for the day!"

"Hey, Timmy!" came two familiar voices. "What's up?"

"Chester! A.J.!" Timmy greeted his friends. "Check out my new *Action Surgery!* game. You can do brain transplants, scrape plaque out of arteries, and even repair a damaged spleen!"

Chapter 2
The Tootie Monster

Timmy left with his friends,
forgetting all about the box of
Wish Tokens. A moment
later, Tootie came looking for him.

"Timmy!" she called. "Timmy Turner,
can you come out and play with me?"

Then Tootie noticed the box of Wish
Tokens on the steps.

"*O-o-o-o!* What's this?" Tootie read the
instructions inside the box: " 'Wish Tokens.
Hold token in hand to make wish.' *O-o-o-o,* I
know what I want!"

Tootie grabbed a shiny token and held it in her hand.

"I wish Timmy Turner could be with me *A-A-A-L-L* the time!" she cried.

"Timmy, this game is great!" said A.J. "I just stitched up a spastic colon!"

"Yeah, but only after I took out the stomach first," said Chester. "Am I an ace action surgeon or what?"

Timmy couldn't answer his
friend. In fact . . .

. . . Timmy was somewhere else!

"Oh, boy!" Tootie squealed. "It worked!"

Timmy thought fast. "Err . . . don't-come-close-Tootie-I-have-a-really-gross-infection-and-I-have-to-go-to-the-doctor-bye!"
he blurted.

Timmy turned and tried to run away—but he couldn't! "What's going on?" he wondered.

Tootie grinned. "You're going to stay with me *a-a-a-ll* the time, Timmy! Know why?"

Timmy gasped, suddenly realizing his mistake.

"My Wish Tokens!"

"No, *my* Wish Tokens," Tootie corrected, grabbing another token. "I wish Timmy would play dollies with me!"

Timmy twitched. Timmy strained. He tried to resist, but the magic was too strong. "Sure, Tootie. Let's play d-d-d-dollies!"

"Yippe-e-e!" cried Tootie.

28

"Wanda!" Timmy whispered. "Cosmo! Help!"

Nothing happened. Then Timmy remembered that his fairy godparents had no extra magic that day. "They can't save me!" he thought. "*A-A-A-A-G-H!!*"

Chapter 4
Playtime with Tootie

"I wuv you, Harold," Tootie said, speaking for her girl doll.

"And I w-w-WUV you, too, Beatrice!" Timmy heard himself say.

Later, Tootie used another Wish Token to make Timmy play jump rope.

"I love Timmy, one-two-three!
I love him, and he loves me!"

Then Tootie used *another* Wish Token to make Timmy play dress-up. "You look divine with that necklace," she told him.

"A-A-A-A-G-H!" Timmy thought.

And finally, Tootie used *another* Wish Token to make Timmy play tea party. "More tea, Mr. Snuggle Bear?" she asked.

It was as if Timmy's mouth had a mind of its own. "Yes, please, Mrs. Flowery Hat Doll," it answered.

Just when Timmy was sure things couldn't get any worse, A.J. and Chester ran up.

"Timmy!" Chester said, pointing at Timmy in a dress, "Dude, what are you *doing?*"

"You disappeared on us," said A.J. "You left us for *this?*"

"Help me!" Timmy wanted to shout. But all he could say was, "Hi! I'm Mr. Snuggle Bear!"

Chester and A.J. burst out laughing.

"Don't you tease my Timmy like that!" said

Tootie angrily. "I wuv my Mr. Snuggle Bear!"

"Hey, don't let us get in the way," A.J. chuckled.

"Yeah," giggled Chester, "have fun, Mr. Snuggle Bear!"

And Timmy's friends left, howling with laughter.

Timmy groaned. How could things get any WORSE? Then he looked up.

"Well, well, well," sneered Vicky, his evil baby-sitter. "Lookie who's playing tea party with my little sister! Let's capture the moment, shall we?"

"Say cheese, loser!" Vicky laughed wickedly.

"*A-A-A-A-G-H!*" Timmy thought helplessly.

To Timmy's surprise, Tootie came to the rescue. She grabbed another Wish Token and said, "I wish Vicky would blow away in a *B-I-I-I-G* wind!" she shouted.

Sure enough, a *B-I-I-I-G* wind blew Vicky far, far away.

"Now's my chance!" Timmy thought, grabbing for a Wish Token.

Chapter 5
Saved—or Not!

"I wish Cosmo and Wanda were here!"
Timmy pleaded.

POOF! His fairy godparents appeared.

"Do you have your wands back yet?"
Timmy asked hopefully.

"Sorry, Timmy," Wanda answered.

"Looks like you used your Wish Token
for nothing!" said Cosmo. "By the way,
nice dress."

Timmy quickly changed back into his clothes.

Then the VERY WORST that could possibly happen happened. "I wish Timmy would kiss me!" Tootie said.

"Oh, I can't bear to look!" cried Wanda turning away.

"Hey, Timmy's a good kisser!" Cosmo
defended. "G-o-o-o-o, Timmy!"

Tootie was so happy! "I love Timmy, I
love Timmy!" she sang. "He's mine forever
and ever and ever!"

Then she looked at Timmy and paused. Having Timmy was a dream come true, but Tootie wanted him to be happy, too.

Timmy was *not* happy.

"Here, Timmy," Tootie said handing him a token. "This is my very last Wish Token. Make a wish that will make *you* happy."

Chapter 6
Good Boy Timmy

Timmy didn't waste any time. "I wish that Tootie had never found my box of Wish Tokens!" he said.

GRANTED!

Timmy was instantly back at his house with his box of Wish Tokens.

"Well, I guess that's that!" said Cosmo. "Things are back to normal—or as close as we ever get."

"Looks like it," agreed Wanda. "Except that I can't help feeling sorry for Tootie."

"Me, too," said Timmy. "She gave up her happiness to make me happy."

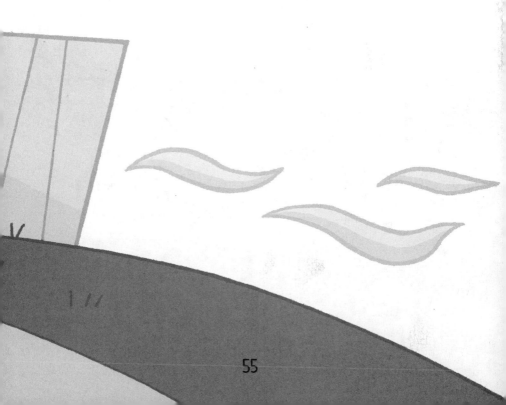

Just then Tootie walked up to Timmy. "Hi, Timmy," she said smiling. "Will you play with me?"

Timmy gathered his courage. "Okay, Tootie," he agreed. "I'll play one game of ball, just to make you happy. One. That's it, okay? One. Just *one*."

"Oh, Timmy!" said Tootie, "I'll love you forever and ever and ever!"

"Yeah, well," Timmy mumbled, "try to keep it to yourself."

"Here," Timmy said, tossing the Wish
Tokens to Cosmo and Wanda. "Go make
yourselves
happy."

"You're a good boy, Timmy," Wanda said.

Tootie grabbed Timmy and dragged him off.

"Now it's *our* turn!" Wanda cried, grabbing a Wish Token.

POOF! Cosmo suddenly found himself pouring tea for Mr. Snuggle Bear.

"One lump or two?" asked Wanda with a twinkle in her eye.

Cosmo twitched. Cosmo strained. He tried to resist, but the magic was too strong . . .